The Painting Of A Dream

A short story by Larry W Jones

The Painting Of A Dream

nce upon a time there lived in a quiet village a handsome young man who
s an artist, a painter of beautiful scenery, landscapes and nature. So talented
s he that the people in his village and in other towns around would come and
y his paintings.

Now, the young artist had a sweetheart, a young lady, two years younger than he, who was as picturesque as his paintings, only more so. Beauteous was her form and pleasant her company.

Today, I wish to paint a new landscape," he said.
...d they both walked to a nearby green field, she helping to
...rry his wooden painting easel, horse-hair brushes and
...lored paints.

His sweetheart stood watching as the young man began painting.

"Oh, the trees are not quite straight," she said. "And maybe the sky should be a darker blue."

"I will correct them both and get it right," he answered. "Then, do you thir the scene will look good?"

h, **there is no doubt**," she said, wondering why he should ask. "After all,
ur paintings are well known as the best around. Whoever buys this one will
nk he is right here in this green field."

ut, **what if this one turns out badly**?" he mused. "There will be no
yer and I will be unhappy."

"No one will be unhappy," she said. "All your paintings show that you tri
hard and did your best. Look beyond the green field where we are." Both of them
stood, arm in arm, and gazed at length at the details of the trees beyond the fiel
the hills in the distance and how the shadows played upon them. It was like a
beautiful dream, a scene like no other and almost unbelievable.

"How can I ever do it justice?" the young man asked. "It would be a grea
honor to try and paint it but, such a disgrace if done badly. Do you think I car
do it well?"

His sweetheart responded, "I know you will if you paint it for people you
love, if you do your very, very best. You must be strong though others are
weak. Then you will go far and your painting will reward you."

he young man thought for a moment, then said "I will paint you into the ene and I will dream of you with each stroke of my brush." Then they looked ce more at the green field, the trees, the hills beyond and the shadows playing on them. The young artist turned to go but his sweetheart lingered, as if ated with the scene. "Dear, are you ready to go now?" asked the artist. "Oh, s. But I almost wish I could stay and be a part of this beautiful setting." hen he escorted her home and they kissed goodbye until a new tomorrow should me.

The next day, rising early, the young artist went to his sweetheart's house to have her assist him again with his artist tools for painting the landscape that s had become so enraptured with the day before. But her mother answered the door and said that her daughter had left the house and would be gone away for awhil "Where did she say she was going?" asked the artist. "She did not say." The mother replied. "Only that she wanted to see a green field somewhere."

"That's odd," thought the artist, as he walked to the village to inquire further Coming upon a villager, he asked, "Have you seen my sweetheart this morning? The villager said to him, "Yes, she strolled by earlier and said that she was going to a woodland beyond a green field. That's all I know."

gain, the artist asked another villager, "Have you seen my sweetheart s morning?" The villager answered "Yes, earlier. She told me that she was ing into some hills beyond a woodland which was beyond a green field." et another villager responded "Yes, she told me all about it and she seemed to fixated on the shadows playing upon the hills. It was as if the shadows were ling her to come and join them. That's all I know."

It was at that moment when the young artist realized the sequence of clues as to where his sweetheart had gone. "She has become part of the landscape and is hidden in the shadows playing upon the hills! I must go and begin to paint t landscape and find her among the shadows." He raced home to gather his painti tools and proceeded to the green field with the trees, hills and shadows beyond.

Now, he knew that his eye must be keen and his touch sure to paint the landscape exactly as in nature, down to every detail. He remembered her answer to his question if the painting would be a good one. "Oh, there is no doubt," sh had said. "After all, your paintings are well known as the best around. Whoeve buys this one will think he is right here in this green field."

ith great concentration he painted with astounding beauty the green field, e trees, the hills and the shadows. But alas! His sweetheart was nowhere to be en in the landscape. What was wrong? Was he only dreaming, a figment of his agination, that she would appear? He gazed intently at the painting and ddenly realized, "The shadows playing upon the hills! They're too dark! I ust lighten the shadows."

On his **p ainter's pallet**, he carefully mixed white, yellow and gold together to reflect the   glow of the sun's rays. With great care he began to paint over the shadows **p** laying upon the hills. But as he lightened the shadows, each brush stroke at **t** he same time formed **an** outline in the middle of the green field. The outl **i** ne appeared more and mor **e** like someone he knew un **t** il it became an exact mi **r** ror image of his sweethe **a** rt. He stood up, amaze **d** at her likeness that he knew he did not paint of his ow **n** free will. Then he thoug **h** t to himself, "Here is my fin **n** ished landscape but my s **w** eetheart is only an imag **e** that I cannot hold. Whe **r** e, oh where can she real **l** y be? Will I ever see her   again in all her fleshly beau ty?"

t that moment he felt a tap on his shoulder. Turning around in the green
eld, there stood, with dreamy eyes and smiling face, his own dear sweetheart in
l her natural beauty. With great excitement and wonder, he took her in his
ms and warmly kissed her.

Where have you been?" he asked her pleadingly. "I slept late this morning"
e replied. "And, oh! I had a wonderful but scary dream last night. I dreamed
at I walked through a green field and into a woodland. Then I climbed some
lls and got lost in the shadows playing upon the hills and you tried to find
e." Intensely, the young man listened as she continued, "I dreamed that the
adows somehow became lighter and were replaced by warm rays from the sun,
d I escaped into a green field."

The young artist looked stunned and wondered if he too had been in the same dream as his sweetheart. It was then that the girl noticed the beautiful landscape painting with her own image standing in the green field. "Oh! I see that you included an image of me in your landscape. How thoughtful of you to go to all that trouble. This one would surely be a masterpiece even without a person in it. I am drawn to this one more than any others you have done."

week later, the long-awaited wedding of the young painter and his sweetheart as held in that same green field. All the local villagers attended as well as any from the towns around, for his skill at painting was of renown in the whole ea.

ſter the wedding a grand reception was given in the village. On display ere, and for sale, were many of the young artist's best landscape paintings.

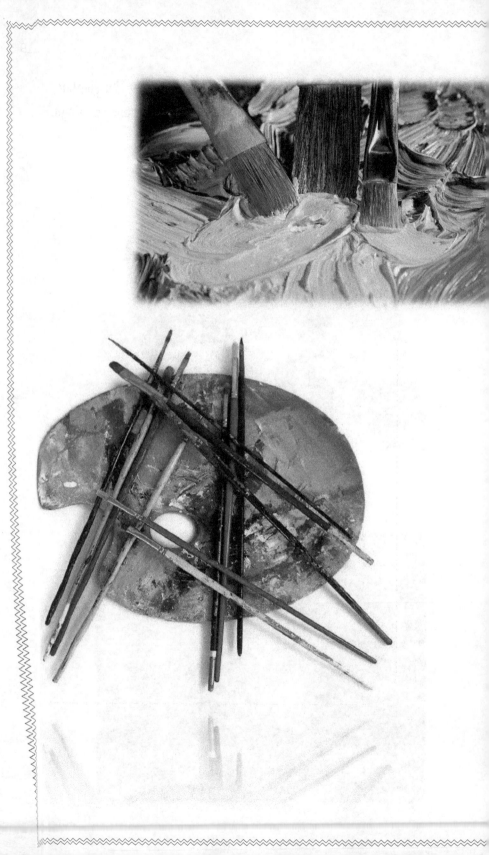

he young artist and his sweetheart bride looked at each other with the me knowing answer. "Thank you sir, for your kindly and generous offer" the tist replied." However, you must choose from one of the others on display. We ll never sell this one because, you see, it is the painting of a dream."

About the author

Larry W Jones is a songwriter, having penned over 7,700 song lyrics. Published in 22 volumes of island themed, country, cowboy, western and bluegrass songs. The entire assemblage is the world's largest collection of lyrics written by an individual songwriter.

As a wrangler on the "Great American Horse Drive", at age 68, he assisted in driving 800 half-wild horses 62 miles in two days, from Winter pasture ground in far NW Colorado to the Big Gulch Ranch outside of Craig Colorado.

His book, "The Oldest Greenhorn", chronicles the adventures and perils in earning the "Gate-to-Gate" trophy belt buckle the hard way.

This book, "The Painting Of A Dream" is his second short-story book.

All his publications are available on lulu.com

CPSIA information can be obtained
at www.ICGtesting.com
Printed in the USA
BVHW011121231220
596341BV00001B/1

9 781716 358975